Fairy-Tale ★ Phonics
Little Red Riding Hood

This book practices:

13 single sounds — also called phonemes

One letter forming one sound:

r (as in red)   w (as in wood)   n (as in neck)   f (as in fast)
h (as in his)   k (as in cake)

Two or more letters forming one sound:

zh (as in treasure)

oo (as in hood) *also spelled -ou*

or (as in sort) *also spelled -oor, -our, -ore*

ear (as in dear)

ie (as in pie) *also spelled -y, -i, i_e, -igh, eye*

ee (as in teeth) *also spelled -ea*

ai (as in tail) *also spelled -ey, -ay, a_e*

2 blends — made by two consonant sounds

Two or more consonants are sounded out individually but are blended together:

gr (as in great)   kw (as in quiet)

How to use this book:

Read aloud and sound out the highlighted sounds on each page

Try the activities at the bottom of each page

Retell the story using the pictures and key sounds on page 23

Practice the sounds with the matching activity on page 24

Once upon a time, there was a little girl who wore a red skirt, red shoes, and a red hood. Her name was Little Red Riding Hood.

Say the words as you spot things beginning with r.

red   rabbit   roof

One day her mother said,
"Grandma is really not well. Can you
run around to see her right away?"

Spell some words with the r sound.

rat   rice   ring   room

3

Emphasize
the w sound
(as in wood)

Red Riding Hood walked through the wood to Grandma's house. A wolf was waiting for her to wander closer — then he jumped out!

Sound out these words with the w sound.

way   win   wig   wool
well   wasp   web

4

"Well, hello," growled the wolf
"Do you want to play?"

"No, thank you. I'm walking
to Grandma's house,"
said Red Riding Hood,
looking worried.

Spell more words beginning with w.

week   wash   worm   window

Sound out
the oo sound
(as in hood)

"Before you leave the wood, why not pick some flowers?" said the wolf.

"I should! What a good idea," said Red Riding Hood.

Spell some words with the oo sound.

would   could   foot   look

6

"What a treasure you are!" said the wolf. "It's a pleasure to meet you." And off he ran.

Sound out these words, which all use the zh sound.

measure   leisure   television
casual   usual

That naughty wolf was soon knocking at Grandma's door. Grandma knew it was not Red Riding Hood, so she hid in the wardrobe.

Sound out these words with the n sound in different positions.

neck   noon   knot   gnaw
funny   line   pan   corn

When the wolf walked in, Grandma was nowhere to be seen. He put on her nightgown and nightcap.

Spell some words beginning with the n sound.

nest   knit   knee   gnome

As the wolf got into bed, Red Riding Hood knocked on the door.

Straight away she saw something wasn't right. She walked across the floor.

Sound out these words, which all use the or sound.

sort   born   horse

shore   score   pour

"Poor Grandma!"
she said. "Your face
looks very odd!"

Spell some more words with the or sound.

fork   short   more   fort

Emphasize
the ear sound
(as in dear)

"Hello, my dear,"
said the wolf.
"Do not fear. Come
and sit near me!"

Complete these sentences with the ear sound.

"What big **ear**s you have, Grandma!" She said
"All the better to h**ear** you with." said the wolf.

12

"My, what big eyes you have, Grandma," said Red Riding Hood.

"All the better to see you with," replied the sly wolf.

Sound out these words with the ie sound.

cry   fly   dry   tie   pie

ride   time   high   night

13

Highlight the
ee sound (as in
teeth)

"And your teeth are huge!"
gasped Little Red Riding Hood.

"All the better to eat you with!"
said the wolf, jumping to his feet.

Red Riding Hood screamed!

Sound out these words with the ee sound.

need   geese   tree   sweet
bead   treat   steam

14

The wolf threw off the nightdress
and Red Riding Hood ran away as fast
as she could, fearing for her life.

Say the words as you spot things with the f sound.

face   fingers   wolf

A woodcutter heard Red Riding Hood screaming. He rushed in, holding his axe.

"I'll have that wolf's tail!" he hollered.

Say the names of the things with the h sound, as you spot them.

hood   hand   head
hedge   handle

Highlight
the ai sound
(as in tail)

But the big gray wolf escaped with his tail. He ran away and never came near Red Riding Hood again — hooray!

Spell some words with the ai sound.

play   stay   rain   paint

17

Then Grandma groaned from inside the wardrobe.

The woodcutter grabbed the handle and let Grandma out.

Sound out some words that begin with the gr blend.

grip   gravy   growl   greedy

grill   group   grass

18

"Thank you!" said Grandma, grinning at the woodcutter, and grabbing Red Riding Hood for a great big hug.

Spell more words beginning with the gr blend.

grid grow green grand

19

Sound out these words, which all use the k sound made by c and k.

cut   cow   card   castle

kiss   key   kitten

"This is cause for cake and a cup of coffee!" said Grandma, and went into the kitchen to put the kettle on and fetch some cupcakes.

Say the words as you spot things beginning with the k sound.

cake stand   cupcake   cup

Focus on the
kw blend
(as in quiet)

The wolf had had quite enough for one day. He went
to live a quiet life deep in the wood and quivered
and quaked whenever he saw Red Riding Hood!

Spell some words beginning with qu.

quit   queen   quilt   quick

Try to **retell** the story using
these key sounds and story images.

red

wolf

door

ears

eyes

teeth

away

Grandma

cupcakes

23

Think of a word that matches the red highlighted **sounds** on each line.

good	could	foot
usual	casual	leisure
knew	nightcap	knock
floor	more	door
eye	high	fly
feet	treat	bead
face	life	wolf
his	hedge	have
quick	queen	quit

You've had fun with phonics! Well done.

Published in 2018 by **Windmill Books**, an Imprint of Rosen Publishing, 29 East 21st Street, New York, NY 10010

Copyright © 2018 Miles Kelly Publishing

All rights reserved. No part of this book may be reproduced in any form without permission in writing from the publisher, except by a reviewer.
Publishing Director: Belinda Gallagher | Creative Director: Jo Cowan | Senior Editor: Fran Bromage | Designer: Jo Cowan
Phonics Consultant: Susan Purcell | Illustrator: Monika Filipina | Concept: Fran Bromage
Acknowlegments: The publishers would like to thank the following sources for the use of their photographs: t = top, b = bottom, rt = repeated throughout.
Cover graphic (t, b) tomka/Shutterstock, (rt) DeepGreen/iStock, (rt) koya979/Shutterstock, (rt) solarbird/Shutterstock

Cataloging-in-Publication Data
Names: Purcell, Susan.
Title: Little Red Riding Hood / Susan Purcell.
Description: New York : Windmill Books, 2018. | Series: Fairy-tale phonics | Includes index.
Identifiers: ISBN 9781508194484 (pbk.) | ISBN 9781508193753 (library bound) | ISBN 9781508194545 (6 pack)
Subjects: LCSH: Little Red Riding Hood (Tale)--Juvenile fiction. | Reading--Phonetic method--Juvenile fiction.
Classification: LCC PZ7.P834 Li 2018 | DDC --dc23

Manufactured in China
CPSIA Compliance Information: Batch BW18WM: For Further Information contact Rosen Publishing, New York, New York at 1-800-237-9932